Teacher's Manual

COMING
OF AGE

Teacher's Manual

SHORT STORIES ABOUT YOUTH & ADOLESCENCE

COMING OF AGE

Bruce Emra

National Textbook Company
NTC a division of *NTC Publishing Group* • Lincolnwood, Illinois USA

1996 Printing

Published by National Textbook Company, a division of NTC Publishing Group.
© 1994 by NTC Publishing Group, 4255 West Touhy Avenue,
Lincolnwood (Chicago), Illinois 60646–1975 U.S.A.
Manufactured in the United States of America.

5 6 7 8 9 0 VP 9 8 7 6 5 4 3

Contents

Part Three
FALLING IN LOVE   29

*Student-written story

Introduction

THE RATIONALE FOR THIS BOOK

Virtually every English/language arts teacher teaches the short story. Why? Because it is an ideally compact and easy-to-manage literary text. All of the literature skills that we want our students to develop—working with theme, characterization, setting, imagery, and tone, to name just a few—can be dealt with as effectively with short stories as with novels. Further, many of the great writers have, of course, written great short stories.

Why *this* collection? We must reach students "where they live," and *Coming of Age* touches upon virtually all aspects of our students' lives. Here in one collection are masterful stories by the best classic and contemporary writers—all of whom deal with the gamut of human experiences faced by young men and women. Literary quality was the primary touchstone for inclusion, but I also considered emotional appeal. That is why this collection is unique. When I was an undergraduate student at New York University, Professor Robert S. Berlin, to whose memory I have dedicated this book, used to talk about teachers choosing reading material for adolescents, and he would quote Hamlet: "What's Hecuba to him or he to Hecuba,/ that he should weep for her?" Professor Berlin meant, "What is so much of what we give our students to read that they should weep for these characters? Our students often can't identify with these characters." With the characters throughout this anthology your students *can* identify.

As a further inspiration for the readers of this book, I have included in each section an award-winning short story by a high school student; these stories are perfect models for your students as they read and write in your classroom. Further, at least one of the professional stories in this collection, Carson McCullers' famous "Sucker," was written when she was seventeen.

The four sections of the anthology tell it all: "Do I Fit In?"; "Families and Friends"; "Falling in Love"; and "Out in the World."

HOW DOES THIS BOOK FIT IN YOUR CURRICULUM?

This book will find its place in many different classrooms. *There is probably half a year's worth of material and work right in this text. Coming of Age* can be used in a course which includes the short story among other genres, of course. But it can also be a key text in, for example, an American literature course. The book can be the essence of theme-oriented courses; I myself plan to use the book in my year-long class entitled "Literature About the Individual."

Wherever teachers are looking for quality literature and wonderful reading and writing activities for their students, this book will find a place.

TEACHING APPARATUS

For every selection there are reader-response questions in "Responding to the Story," critical thinking activities in "Exploring the Author's Craft," and copious writing opportunities in "Writing Workshop." For many of the stories we have included a creative "Alternative Media Response," encouraging students to work with art and video, for example. Almost all of these questions and activities are based on what I know works in the classroom.

This Teacher's Manual will provide you with many suggestions about how best to use *Coming of Age*. Of course, true to the spirit of reader-response theory, *your* unique individual responses to these stories will determine the types of classes you create.

I hope this anthology will "grab" students—and teachers—on an emotional level. The stories collected here are about your students, about young men and women finding their places in the world.

Bruce Emra

Part One
Do I Fit In?

Eleven
Sandra Cisneros

INTRODUCING THE STORY

Ask students whether they can remember some past birthday. Was it a happy or unhappy day? What could make a birthday an unhappy occasion? Share your own remembrances of a birthday, if possible. Then assign "Eleven," a story told in the first person about someone remembering a birthday.

RESPONDING TO THE STORY

1. *What does the narrator mean when she says . . . ?* All of us are one age by the calendar, but part of us contains all the ages we have passed through—and we can often remember them quickly. We go up and down; how quickly we can be immature seven-year-olds again, or maybe innocent, trusting, wide-eyed four-year-olds again. This is Sandra Cisneros' insight in this story. Let your students talk about whether they accept the idea. Have them give examples.

2. *Why does the narrator wish this day . . . ?* The red sweater plopped on her desk by Mrs. Price mortifies our narrator. And there is nothing worse than being embarrassed in front of one's classmates. This particular embarrassment happens right on Rachel's birthday so it takes on particular importance.

3. *Are the narrator's feelings this day . . . ?* The "interactive" language arts teacher today is a facilitator—someone who serves to get the students motivated: speaking, writing, sharing—in short, using language arts skills. A good teacher will elicit comments in which students speak of their own moments of mortification in school. Teachers who share their own stories become real and nonthreatening to students. A classroom which employs "reader response to literature" needs to be one of great trust and warmth for the sharing to follow. Many of the questions in *Coming of Age* ask students to use their memories and feelings as well as their intellects.

EXPLORING THE AUTHOR'S CRAFT

1. *What is the narrator of "Eleven" like? Describe her personality.* This narrator is both animated and sensitive. She's bright—she recognizes that no one is simply

one age; we're a combination of everything that has gone on before. And she's open with her feelings. Not only does she cry in front of all her classmates but she tells all of us about it. Are your students able to be as open with their feelings?

2. *Is this an accurate portrait of someone turning eleven . . . ?* First, your students will have to decide what Rachel is like. Then they will have to decide if other eleven-year-old girls are similar. This should provoke a good discussion, and every class discussing this question will get different responses.

3. *In a story told from a first-person point of view . . .* No, we get only a limited view from a first-person narrator. Everything is told from the viewpoint of that one person. The narrator isn't a fair reporter of what other people are thinking; how would he or she really know? Help your students realize this limitation of a first-person narration.

WRITING WORKSHOP

Create a first-person narrator and tell about something . . . Try to give models of what might be satisfactory submissions in this Writing Workshop. Create files of the best of this year's papers for use next year with the book. Give class time for students to talk with each other about what they want to do and to share what they have attempted. This is to be a collaborative effort, one that produces pleasure and satisfaction.

The Secret Lion
Alberto Alvaro Ríos

INTRODUCING THE STORY

Some students may have memories of special or forbidden neighborhood places they knew as children, places unknown or ordinary to an adult but filled with meaning for a child. The Southwest setting will be familiar to many students. For those classes unfamiliar with the Southwest, establish the geographical and climatic setting for the story, noting that non-native plants can thrive only with irrigation. Ask students to be ready to discuss the meaning of the title.

RESPONDING TO THE STORY

1. *Why do the narrator and his friend . . . go to the arroyo?* Simple. "It was the one place we were not supposed to go. So we did." Have students find the lines in the text to answer this question. Then go beyond the text to the students' lives. Every adolescent will be able to identify with this theme; let them talk about it.

2. *How is the missing ball "like that place, that whole arroyo"?* Ríos gives us the answer to this question right in his text: "Couldn't tell anything about it, didn't understand what it was, didn't have a name for it. It just felt good . . ." Have your students talk this through; do they know what the author means?

3. *What does the sentence "They were still mountains then" mean?* "They were still mountains then" because the boys were still boys—"since everything looks bigger the smaller a man is." Ask your students if they know this experience. The sharing of universal human experiences such as these can bring a class together; when the atmosphere is trusting, more sharing can occur.

4. *In a paragraph, describe the way . . .* Research shows that students often learn more from their peers than from their teachers. Let students share their paragraphs in class. The audience for student writing mustn't be limited to the teacher; teach students that there is a wide audience for what they write.

5. *Why do you think the story has the title it does?* Elicit student responses to this question. Don't give your own thoughts. This story is about being twelve and seeing the world through a twelve-year-old's eyes; a teacher is too old to give a response here.

EXPLORING THE AUTHOR'S CRAFT

Tone *is an author's attitude about his or her subject . . .* Tone is a difficult concept for students to deal with. Will the students see the tongue-in-cheek (if they even know that phrase) tone of this story by an adult recalling the limited view of the world he had at twelve? The tone isn't condescending; it's too tender and respectful of twelve-year-olds for that. The story certainly has regret in it—regret for the innocence we all lose. Ask students to find textual evidence for whatever tone or tones they find in the story.

WRITING WORKSHOP

Imagine that you are one of the boys . . . Obviously there's no right or wrong response here. Write the nouns and adjectives on the board. Let students work individually on poems and then let them share what they have done. Do the poems maintain the same tone as "The Secret Lion"?

ALTERNATE MEDIA RESPONSE

1. *Draw a map that captures the world these boys . . .* This should be fun and might appeal to those learners who do better with graphic representations than with abstract concepts; we don't all learn the same way. Let students have fun with this. Give them fifteen or twenty minutes to work at it, and then share some maps with the class. Be sure that students can justify the decisions they made in creating their drawings.

2. *Write a script for a video dramatization . . .* If no one has access to a video camera, then share the scripts. Ideally, however, the scripts will be filmed or videotaped and the story will come alive. The story should be told through the words and actions of the characters, and the creators should stay true to the spirit and tone of "The Secret Lion." Encourage students to include camera direction along with the script.

A Mother in Mannville
Marjorie Kinnan Rawlings

INTRODUCING THE STORY

Remind students of the topic of the first part of the text, "Do I Fit In?" Ask: Of all human needs such as need for food, shelter, clothing, meaningful work, and so on, where would you rank the need to fit in? Near the top of a list of ten human needs or closer to the bottom? What kind of behavior might this need create in people? Have students read to discover how Jerry tries to achieve his need to fit in.

RESPONDING TO THE STORY

1. *List four different things Jerry does that convince . . .* Here are four; there are more. (a) Jerry says he'll take whatever the woman wants to give him to cut the wood; (b) he offers to pay to get the ax fixed; (c) he makes certain the woman has dry firewood in case of bad weather; (d) he fixes the walk to the cabin. He was required to do none of these things.

2. *Where in the story is the first reference . . . ?* When the narrator tells Jerry, "I am leaving tomorrow," he doesn't answer. Then we learn that he didn't eat his meal the next day. Also, most uncharacteristically, he didn't light the boiler at the orphanage. We are meant to realize that the narrator's announcing that she is leaving has affected Jerry deeply.

   Let students talk about their feelings regarding the last moments of this story. As I was writing this material I asked my wife if she had ever read "A Mother in Mannville." "Oh, yes," she said. "Marjorie Kinnan Rawlings. I hated the woman at the end of the story." It turns out that my wife hated the narrator for abandoning Jerry; my wife's motherly feelings made this story memorable to her. Your students may have some strong reactions too.

3. *What do you think were Jerry's reasons . . . ?* There are no right or wrong answers here. Let the conversation proceed.

4. *What did you feel as the story ended . . . ?* This is pure reader response; students must be allowed their own natural reactions. Those reactions can't be helped, of course, or controlled.

EXPLORING THE AUTHOR'S CRAFT

1. *The term* **irony** *refers to the difference between . . .* The ultimate sad irony in this story is summarized in the last eight words: "He has no mother. He has no skates." We were led to expect something quite different; we had come to believe Jerry's words about the mother and about the skates.

2. *Why does the author end with the blunt declarative sentences . . . ?* This ending is one of the most dramatic we could ever imagine in literature. The shock the reader feels simulates exactly what the narrator feels.

WRITING WORKSHOP

Think of someone you know or a character you have read about. . . . Creating the two or three incidents that reveal character will help students realize the heart of fiction—showing and not telling. We came to believe in Jerry because he had been painted almost a saint. (Early in the story we learn that "a light came over him, as though the setting sun had touched him with the same suffused glory with which it touched the mountains.")

As these papers are shared in class, help students to point out what makes the strongest papers work. Not only will students receive pleasure seeing and hearing each other's work (and maybe finding their own praised), they will also be learning one of the critical elements of good writing—the use of specific incidents to dramatize a generalization.

ALTERNATE MEDIA RESPONSE

Draw or paint a picture of the narrator's face as you imagine . . . It will be interesting to see what certain students do with this task. One can imagine some sensitive and moving illustrations.

Raymond's Run
Toni Cade Bambara

INTRODUCING THE STORY

Either read or have the first few paragraphs of the story read aloud. Then ask students to describe the narrator briefly, based on what she reveals about herself. Is she appealing? If so, why? How is the voice of the narrator of this story different from the voice of the narrator of "Eleven"?

RESPONDING TO THE STORY

1. *This story could have been placed in the "Families and Friends" unit . . .* Squeaky seems to fit in her neighborhood. Her success at running gives her an image, an identity, a place. The way she speaks to us in the story and the way she tells us she speaks on the street show a seemingly confident person filled with a kind of bravado. She may have certain insecurities, but she seems at home with the neighborhood and the people in it.

2. *Do you think the author was able to create a believable . . . voice?* You'll get a variety of reactions to this question. Some nonurban students may never have heard a voice like Squeaky's. Some urban students may say the voice sounds real. Ask: If the main character had been a boy, how might the story have changed? Good speculation will produce a lively discussion and maybe a writing assignment with a first-person voice. (See the Writing Workshop for this story.)

3. *Do you agree with Hazel Elizabeth Deborah Parker . . . ?* Do the boys in your class take one view and the girls another? Squeaky's ultimate comment on girls is devastating—that they aren't real, that they're too busy being other things all the time. (Squeaky, of course, could be accused of not being totally natural but creating a tough, cool voice for herself.) What do your students think of this conclusion? Can they give examples from the world *they* know? And then ask: Are boys just as unnatural, too?

EXPLORING THE AUTHOR'S CRAFT

Authors use a variety of techniques to define a character . . . Squeaky's concern for Raymond helps us see her compassionate side. Simply, she loves her brother and doesn't want him to be ridiculed by others. She's able to get outside herself only when it comes to her brother. Raymond's presence in the story helps to explain how Squeaky developed her attitudes toward life.

WRITING WORKSHOP

Listen carefully to the way various people around you speak. . . . Give the students paper and let them go. They will surprise you; they will startle you. Adolescents can write dialogue more easily than they can write poetry or narration; they know the voices of themselves and their friends.

Have these "voices" performed aloud. Several could be combined into a kind of script, a dramatization that represents the world as your students see it in the week (in the history of the world) in which they did this writing. These creations are valid social documents about the time in which they were written.

Two Kinds
Amy Tan

INTRODUCING THE STORY

Ask students to suggest (as someone writes on the chalkboard) the qualities needed to be a champion. Do these qualities apply to success in any field of endeavor? Have the word *prodigy* defined (i.e., a highly talented child) and discuss whether natural talent is necessary to being a champion. Is it worthwhile to try to achieve something for which one has no natural talent? Have students ever been prodded to succeed at something for which they felt they had no talent? Why? How does one know whether one has a talent for something? Ask students to read to discover the reasons for Jing-mei's failure to live up to her mother's expectations.

RESPONDING TO THE STORY

1. *Why do you think the narrator started performing "listlessly" and decided . . .* This is a great story about parent-child tensions and the psychological tugs-of-war that occur. The narrator at first likes the idea of becoming a prodigy. ("In all my imaginings I was filled with a sense that I would soon become *perfect.*") But when she doesn't meet her mother's expectations (". . . after seeing my mother's disappointed face once again, something inside of me began to die"), she turns the other way: "I won't let her change me, I promised myself. I won't be what I'm not." Have your students find the excerpts to back up whatever statements they make; always go to the text.

   Maybe down deep the narrator didn't like failing and letting her mother down and thus resisted any goals the mother set. Does this psychological explanation make sense to your students, who could be having similar feelings right now? The discussion is underway.

2. *What does the mother say is her reason for pushing her daughter to take piano lessons?* The mother says she "only ask you be your best. For you sake." These are sentiments every parent has uttered. The interesting part of the students' writing will be whether they think the mother's reasons are valid.

3. *Why does the mother say to Auntie Lindo, "Our problem worser than yours . . ."?* The mother seems to be bragging. She wants to emphasize that Jing-mei is talented and dedicated.

4. *What are the final outrageous "magic" words the narrator says to her mother . . . ?* "Then I wish I wasn't your daughter. I wish you weren't my mother," the girl first shouts. Who of us hasn't uttered a variation of this attack? The "awful side" in all of us (despite Jing-mei's saying it "felt good" to utter the words) can say some pretty rotten things. When her mother doesn't collapse from the first words, Jing-mei takes it one step further: "Then I wish I'd never been born! I wish I were dead. Like them [the babies the mother had lost in China]." This finally defeats her mother.

5. *How do "Pleading Child" and "Perfectly Contented" have a double meaning in the story . . . ?* There is artistry in the titles Amy Tan has chosen for the two piano pieces. Ask the students if it is significant that "Pleading Child" was "shorter but slower" and "Perfectly Contented" was "longer, but faster." When was Jing-mei a "pleading child" and when was she "perfectly contented"? Do the two phrases capture two key aspects of Jing-mei ("they were two halves of the same song")? Let your students go with the conversation; don't guide them too much here. Keep going back to the text.

EXPLORING THE AUTHOR'S CRAFT

*A **simile** compares two things that have common characteristics but are essentially unlike each other. . . .* Give the students time to do this in class. Similes won't come easily; creating them requires a new way of seeing *and* writing. Let students share their similes in groups. Have students articulate the two elements that are common in the unlike objects or things. Help students see whether their similes are fresh or merely repeats of ones they have heard or read. By writing and analyzing, students can become excellent critics.

WRITING WORKSHOP

Tell about an incident of your own growing up . . . These scenes with dialogue can be done in class or for homework. It is difficult to imagine that any teenager would say that the theme of parental (or other adult) expectations hasn't occurred in his or her life. Share the papers; the sharing humanizes the classroom, and students will see that they're not the only ones to have experienced tensions at home.

ALTERNATE MEDIA RESPONSE

1. *Write and perform a piece of music . . .*
2. *Create and perform a dance . . .*
3. *With others . . . dramatize a segment of this story . . .* These are creative opportunities for your students. Isn't this what the dynamic language arts classroom should be—a place where students not only study and analyze other people's creations but have the chance to produce their own?

Louisa, Please Come Home
Shirley Jackson

INTRODUCING THE STORY

If students are familiar with Shirley Jackson's work, they will need no motivation to read. If they are not, ask them to read to discover why the author achieved a reputation for writing bizarre and frightening stories.

RESPONDING TO THE STORY

1. *How did you feel while you were reading this story?* Get reactions from as many students as possible. And if you're discussing this story in period three, let's say, don't expect the responses to be the same as they were in period one; nothing is predictable in an open classroom, and that adds to the excitement, energy, and fun. Certainly students will respond to the strangeness of this story. Don't let them be limited to the literal: "Of course a parent would recognize his or her child."
2. *Did you like Louisa/Lois? Did you hate her . . . ?* Again, this is pure reader response, and the different responses will reflect the uniqueness of the individuals in your classroom. Students should find touching the simple expression of what seems to be sincere emotions: "I realized that all I wanted was to stay . . ."
3. *Give your reactions to Louisa's parents, her sister, and Paul.* A good debate may ensue, based on the values and experiences of the people in your room. When we learn of Paul's two earlier deliveries of "Louisa," in anticipation of a reward, it's difficult to have much sympathy for him.
4. *Why do you think Carol was at the house when Louisa returned . . . ?* This question is open to speculation. It's appropriate for the tone and tension in the story that another odd thing has occurred: there is no mention of why Carol isn't away somewhere in her new married life. Perhaps it's because the family is in crisis; Carol is needed to be there.

5. *Does the author provide a motivation for Louisa's leaving home? If so, what is it?* The narrator tells us that she took a certain pleasure in hoping to spoil Carol's wedding. In a larger sense we might say that somehow Louisa's leaving was an existential statement about her life: she was in control of it, and she was making the break.

EXPLORING THE AUTHOR'S CRAFT

Discuss what makes this story different from the five stories . . . Any story written by Shirley Jackson is going to be different from everyone else's stories. The first five stories in this collection are much more grounded in reality than is this one. Yes, teenagers run away from home, but few come home to this kind of reception. What did author Shirley Jackson have in mind? We can only speculate. Jackson created modern-day horror stories—think of "The Lottery"—and turned reality upside down. On the one hand, we might wonder what kind of parents wouldn't eagerly welcome home their long-absent daughter. On the other hand, having been fooled twice by Paul, Mr. and Mrs. Tether are highly wary when he brings a third girl claiming to be Louisa. Maybe their behavior is psychologically sound; they are protecting themselves from more hurt.

Mr. Tether says, "My daughter was younger than you are," and he is certainly correct in that. He only remembers his daughter as she was, three painful years earlier. Maybe Shirley Jackson wanted little more than to play with the reader and turn things upside down on her protagonist, Louisa. Just when Louisa seems in charge, she is rejected in her own household and must always live with the cry, "Louisa, please come home."

The Tethers are certainly on a tether; all their lives are "tied or constrained within a certain limit," as one definition of the word has it. This family—maybe all families—can never escape the bonds they all share.

WRITING WORKSHOP

Here's your chance for some unconventionality. Working with a small group . . . Adolescents love the bizarre. See if your students can create a story both believable and unique, as we might characterize "Louisa, Please Come Home."

The Man in the Casket
Beth Cassavell

INTRODUCING THE STORY

Ask how many students have been to a funeral. After a show of hands, tell them that this student-written story is about a girl's memory of and reaction to the death of her grandfather. Her reactions may surprise students. Ask the students as they read to note the words the author uses to create the tone of the story.

RESPONDING TO THE STORY

1. *Is this reaction of a granddaughter to her grandfather's death believable . . . ?* Many students will acknowledge feeling awkward at a funeral with an open casket. Many may also acknowledge having a variety of feelings at the death of someone close to them; all of our feelings are not as noble as we might wish. And students might understand why the narrator cried—finally.

2. *Explain how you interpret the last paragraph of the story.* The narrator's "humanness," to use her word, runs through this story. Her coldness may be believable. Her resentments are authentic. Her scorn of hypocrisy is identifiable. She *does* have a tender side—much as she tries not to show it—which she reveals when she tells us that she saw her grandfather cry and had "almost a feeling of curiosity" about his life. All of these things come together at the side of the casket. Maybe her grandfather *did* love her, despite her "bratty" rejection of that possibility. "I stopped. I realized. I cried."

EXPLORING THE AUTHOR'S CRAFT

1. **Diction** *is an author's choice of words or phrases . . .* It is worthwhile trying to analyze how Beth Cassavell—a sixteen year old when this story was written—achieved her effects in this story. For one thing, she fools all of our expectations. Young people typically write of grandparents with praise; but here everything is turned around. Early in the story we learn of a "cluttered" "cold and grey" funeral parlor. The walls are "threatening" and "ugly with ornate trimming" and the "Corinthian columns added to the inelegance." The author creates a negative tone through description of the setting. Have your students cite words and phrases throughout the story that contribute to this negative tone.

2. *Many young people write sincerely and frankly, yet the work fails to have emotional power . . .* Virtually the entire story maintains the tone that Beth Cassavell established in the first paragraph. We are surprised at the ending—

just as we were with the ending of "A Mother in Mannville"—because everything that preceded it was of a different tone. This is masterful storytelling. If Beth Cassavell had praised her grandfather throughout the story and then told us how she cried over his coffin, who would have felt any surprise? Instead, this story has many surprises—and much honesty. The end is moving, perhaps because we were unprepared for it. Credit the skill of the author to use tone to set us up for an emotional wallop.

WRITING WORKSHOP

Write a poem, essay, or story about a grandparent-grandchild relationship. Taking a page from Beth Cassavell's story, mandate that, whatever they tell, your students be honest, not romantic and sentimental. Grandparents come in all different shapes, sizes, and personalities; help your students bring those people alive on the page.

RESPONDING TO PART ONE

1. *All but one of these stories is told from the point of view* . . . "A Mother in Mannville" is certainly appropriate in this section. Jerry, sadly, seems to fit in only in the orphanage. When he has started to feel comfortable with a substitute mother—the narrator—and with her dog, she abruptly announces she is leaving. His world is shattered again. We learn that he has lied. We learn that he is much more complex than we might have thought. We worry about what will happen to him. Will he ever "fit in" in life?

2. *A first-person story is compelling when the narrator has unusual experiences* . . . Is there a variety of "most interesting" stories among your students? There should be. Be sure your students articulate their reasons for preferring certain stories.

Part Two
Families and Friends

Adjö Means Good-bye
Carrie A. Young

INTRODUCING THE STORY

Delay discussion of prejudice until after the story is read. Instead, ask students what advice they would give to someone who wants to make friends in a new school or neighborhood. Discuss briefly whether people of different backgrounds and upbringing can be friends. Can people of different religions and colors be friends? Have students read to discover the reasons for the failure of a friendship.

RESPONDING TO THE STORY

1. *Explain why Marget was the narrator's "first love and first hurt."* Marget is a close friend of the narrator—her first love—but also the person who introduced her to prejudice and the cruelties of the world. Thus Marget is also the narrator's first hurt.

2. *What does the author mean when she . . . ?* The experience of the birthday party touched the narrator profoundly and she wonders if it affected Marget at all. Probably not, since Marget wasn't the one hurt. Does she have her own life? Does she make her own decisions instead of being directed by others—a pawn— who have their own agendas?

EXPLORING THE AUTHOR'S CRAFT

The narrator implies from the beginning that this story . . . We are told in the second paragraph that this story will have sadness in it. "Marget was both my first love and first hurt" is foreshadowing. In paragraph five there is more foreshadowing as we read the word *dark* and learn about Marget's apprehensiveness as she "really looked at my brother when she was visiting me." Then the narrator writes that " . . . a strange fear gripped me."

In the scene where the narrator is scolded for picking the flowers, there is further foreshadowing as we are led to believe something bad might happen. Even though the scene ends happily, we are prepared for sadness ahead. When people don't arrive at the party, we worry. And then we are bluntly told by the narrator, "How does a child of ten describe a sense of foreboding . . . ?" We start to steel ourselves for what is to come. The paragraph when the girls drop hands is especially painful and indicative of the truth that is about to be revealed—that the narrator's color is unacceptable. Can your students find other moments of foreshadowing in this masterful story?

WRITING WORKSHOP

1. *Does prejudice still exist in our society today . . . ?* Be sure your students include anecdotes and examples in their essays; generalizations won't do. Teach the meaning of the word *anecdote* and be sure students don't confuse it with *antidote,* a common student mistake.

2. *Write a diary entry from Marget's point of view . . .* These should be fascinating to share. See whether students feel that Marget is suffering from being made a "pawn."

A Christmas Memory
Truman Capote

INTRODUCING THE STORY

Put the following sentences on the chalkboard and discuss which gives the clearest picture of an old person:

He was very old with white hair, and he limped.

He was about eighty-five years old and walked with a cane.

His hand on the ivory-headed cane was as wrinkled as a raisin, and his hair was the color of cotton.

Give students class time to try one of these writing assignments. They need not use figurative language, but they must attempt to use precise, specific words to create an image in three or four sentences.

Describe the tallest person you know.

Describe your favorite relative.

Describe the sky today.

Describe the sounds in the classroom.

Describe the feel of hot beach sand on your bare feet.

Ask students to note Capote's choice of words in this story about a family member who was also a close friend.

RESPONDING TO THE STORY

1. *The narrator says of his "sixty-something" cousin and friend* . . . One of the charms of his friend involves her childlike, innocent ways. At sixty-something she is still able to imagine, play, and have fun with a seven-year-old. It's still exciting for her to make thirty fruit cakes every holiday season. She gets excited about entering contests. Two years earlier she and the narrator, Buddy, created a Fun and Freak Museum in the backyard. It's her attitude that convinces Buddy that "she is still a child" and "Not funny. Fun. More fun than anybody." This is the ultimate tribute.

2. *Considering the things the narrator's friend has never done and what she has done* . . . This question will test your students' value systems. In our contemporary society, with "global village" access to everything, will any adolescent state that being able to tame hummingbirds and tell ghost stories are desirable abilities? Let your students debate the topic; no answer is correct or incorrect.

3. *The narrator's friend tells him "I've always thought . . ."* The friend concludes that "seeing Him" amounts to being aware of all the wonderful things that are around us in *this* world. On the particular day she tells this to Buddy, we're told, "That things as they are"—her hand circles in a gesture that gathers clouds and kites and grass and Queenie pawing earth over her bone—"just what they've always seen, was seeing Him."

4. *Why do you think the narrator included more happy events . . . ?* Truman Capote's strategy—if he thought it out that far—was a sound one in terms of storytelling. This story ultimately moves us (one would have to be a rock to remain untouched by this narration) because we come to care so much for this unusual friendship which is captured in so many happy moments. We are won over by the happy moments, so the sad ones catch us unprepared and we are moved. This formula works for much fiction.

EXPLORING THE AUTHOR'S CRAFT

The narrator's memory serves him well, for he is able to . . . This might be the most significant assignment in the book. If you can help your students understand how crucial details are in *any* piece of writing, you have achieved something. If you can go one step further and actually have your students *want* to write with details, then you are Teacher of the Year. "A Christmas Memory" is a perfect model of the effectiveness of concrete details in a piece of writing. We truly are transported to the time and places of this story because Capote describes or names every little aspect of significant moments. Students can do that too (perhaps not with Capote's lyricism) if they are willing to take the time.

WRITING WORKSHOP

Capture in two- or three-hundred words some moment that brought . . . With this assignment students can employ the techniques Capote demonstrated. Concrete details make a piece of writing authentic instead of bland and unconvincing.

ALTERNATE MEDIA RESPONSE

Find or take a series of photographs that tell this story . . . Here is a chance for your students to (a) show that they understand the story; and (b) demonstrate their own creativity. Black-and-white or sepia plates might best capture the old-time feel of this story.

The Scarlet Ibis
James Hurst

INTRODUCING THE STORY

Read the first few paragraphs of the story aloud; ask students to make a few predictions about the story and then to read to discover how sound their predictions were.

RESPONDING TO THE STORY

1. *Explain the role of the narrator's pride in this story* . . . Several times in this story the narrator tells us that his pride gets in the way of a normal relationship with his brother. The narrator pushes Doodle to accomplish certain physical feats and become as normal as possible so that the narrator won't be embarrassed to be a disabled boy's brother.

2. *James Hurst created a sympathetic character in Doodle* . . . First, Doodle's frailties endear him to us; we feel sorry for him. Then we see how tender he is toward the dead ibis, a side of Doodle that makes him irresistible to the reader. He never shows resentment about his fate but, rather, a heightened sensitivity to all life around him. Students can probably find other references.

3. *How is Doodle's death foreshadowed?* Doodle's death is foreshadowed right from the first paragraph as we read about "our dead." We read about the coffin in the attic and learn that the go-cart is "still there," but a careful reading will reveal the implication that the "mahogany coffin" is gone. The whole extended scene with the scarlet ibis and Doodle's extraordinary identification with it foreshadows his death. "Doodle's hands were clasped at his throat" in this scene,

again giving us a sense of foreboding. That we are meant to pay attention to this scene is clear from the story's title.

EXPLORING THE AUTHOR'S CRAFT

1. *The* **climax** *or climactic moment is the turning point in a story . . .* The climactic moment, it can be argued, occurs when the narrator makes the decision to keep running ahead and not respond to Doodle's pleas, "Brother, Brother, don't leave me! Don't leave me!" The theme of the narrator's "cruelty" and "spite" emerge again at this critical moment in the story.

   One reason that the story has become a modern-day classic is that many people believe that the narrator's actions are very human.

2. *A* **symbol** *is something that represents something else . . .* Readers will note how carefully author James Hurst draws parallels between Doodle and the red bird that dies in the family's yard. Not only do they look alike, their deaths are similar. Doodle's exoticism parallels that of the scarlet ibis which struggles but cannot survive in his environment.

WRITING WORKSHOP

Perceptive readers may have noticed the frequent references to . . . Nothing in this story appears on the page by chance. This was author Hurst's first published story (in 1960) and he crafted it carefully. Red, of course, is the color of blood, and it is an intense color. It is a perfect symbol in this story. Some students may say that red symbolizes life, others that it symbolizes death here.

Sucker
Carson McCullers

INTRODUCING THE STORY

Write the following line from Sophocles (*Oedipus Rex*) on the chalkboard: "The greater griefs are those we cause ourselves." Ask students to speculate on this thought and then read to discover how it might apply to the story "Sucker."

RESPONDING TO THE STORY

1. *How did you feel about Sucker when the story ended . . . ?* Are your students pleased that Sucker stood up to Pete? Adolescents might very well know the

feeling of continually being put down by somebody and wanting revenge. Sucker gets revenge in this story, so much revenge that his whole personality has changed. If students feel sympathetic toward Sucker at the story's end, it's because they've been offended at Pete's treatment of him and can identify with Sucker.

2. *"If a person admires you a lot you despise him . . ."* (a) Pete feels neglected by Maybelle and keeps pursuing her, perhaps because his feelings are hurt, perhaps because of his pride—he has to win. He admires her. Sucker looks up to Pete, and Pete doesn't care. The thinking behind this statement is "anybody who really looks up to me isn't worth pursuing; the challenge is in those who don't care about me." There's a lot of valid psychology in this one sentence, which was written when Carson McCullers was a perceptive seventeen year old. (b) I've found over the years that discussion of this quotation provokes much comment; most adolescents agree with McCullers' analysis of human behavior and have their own examples.

3. *Do you see any similarities between the narrator of "Sucker" . . . ?* Both narrators let pride affect their lives. In "The Scarlet Ibis" the narrator is embarrassed about having a disabled brother. In "Sucker" the narrator's pride is hurt when he loses Maybelle to a boy in a yellow roadster. In both cases a brother gets hurt because of the pride.

There are some obvious differences between the two narrators; the supporting characters and the plot lines are different in the two stories, naturally. Though someone may say that a death occurs in only one of the stories, there is the death of the old, innocent, loving Sucker.

EXPLORING THE AUTHOR'S CRAFT

This story was carefully structured. Explain how . . . The narrator looks up to Maybelle but she rejects him, finally saying that she never cared a rap about him. Sucker looks up to Pete, and Pete, in his hurt over Maybelle, rejects Sucker in the same way. He almost uses the same words: "Don't think I give a darn about a dumb-bunny like you."

WRITING WORKSHOP

In any form you wish—story, essay, poem, or short script—create a written work . . . Most of your students will know about the tensions that occur between or among siblings. The key thing for you to do is to help students tell their story using incidents or moments that dramatize the relationship. Don't let your students *generalize;* instead, make them *particularize* using incidents.

A Private Talk with Holly
Henry Gregor Felsen

INTRODUCING THE STORY

Ask what the class thinks is the biggest obstacle to getting along with a parent or guardian. Ask students to read to try to discover the reasons for the apparently successful relationship in this story.

RESPONDING TO THE STORY

Explain what each character felt during this talk out on the water . . . By the time this story ends, the father is crushed. Holly, surviving the awkwardness of having to tell her father something he doesn't want to hear, is relieved.

Students reading this story may feel a bit for the father, but they're more likely to identify with the situation that Holly is in; your students have probably felt the need to break free and go out on their own. What the writer says in the last paragraph is probably true; an adolescent won't know what the father is feeling in this story "until some day in the future . . ."

EXPLORING THE AUTHOR'S CRAFT

Every story must have a **conflict,** *a struggle between two opposing forces . . .* The superficial conflict is between a daughter and her father, both of whom care for each other. The bigger conflict involves Life with a capital "L." Inevitably, Holly will have to leave home and be out on her own; the fishing trips and all the sharing between father and daughter will have to diminish in frequency and, probably, finally end. The father in this story is upset to see that ending coming so soon, "without a word of warning."

Holly must have a conflict within herself: "How do I say this to Dad? Should I suggest it?" And the father has his own conflict between his emotional need to be able to share time with his daughter and his intellect which must tell him that he has to let his daughter "walk out into the grown-up world forever."

WRITING WORKSHOP

A parent might understand this story more than a teenager does . . . How *does* a parent feel in certain situations? Let your class brainstorm this assignment as a group. Are there situations in which students see that parents actually *do* have a valid point of view? These should be interesting poems and stories to share—even with parents or guardians.

ALTERNATE MEDIA RESPONSE

1. *Draw a picture of any scene . . .*
2. *Create a fifteen-minute film or video that tells this story . . .* Why should a language arts or English class only study other people's works? Here's where your class can really come alive—when your students become writers and artists, too.

Shaving
Leslie Norris

INTRODUCING THE STORY

Ask students to give their opinions on what it means to be mature. Is maturity only a matter of age? Is it a matter of being able to do what one couldn't do at an earlier age, such as getting a driver's license? How do people show that they are mature? Is being aware of and responsive to the needs of others one sign of maturity? At what age do people gradually become aware of and responsive to others' needs? Have students recall the story "Sucker" and determine when the narrator became mature. Assign "Shaving" and ask students to be ready to discuss the relationship between the father and son in the story.

RESPONDING TO THE STORY

1. *How does the shaving bowl represent two different parts of . . . ?* Barry has especially fond memories of his father shaving "in the days of his health." The shaving bowl has served Barry's father longer than Barry has been alive, and now Barry will use that bowl and his father's razor to shave the dying man. The shaving bowl adds a poignancy to the story.

2. *The author describes the preparing and putting away of the shaving tools . . .* The words "ritualistic" and "ceremonial" are often associated with a religious observance or custom, and this association helps define Barry's attitude toward his father. The circumstances surrounding the act of shaving are almost formal in nature and imply a reverence for his father's feelings.

3. *What prompts the father to "let go all his authority . . ."* First, the man is dying. He has no choice but to let his son shave him. But he loves his son and sees the love being returned by Barry in the tender act of shaving. Because of the sharp razor the act has danger implied in it; but the intimacy of helping one's

father who "feels dirty with all that beard on him" creates a beautiful and loving moment to which Barry's father surrenders. The boy is now a man and, in a sense, has taken over for the father, and the father is willing to see the mantle passed.

EXPLORING THE AUTHOR'S CRAFT

1. *Writers often imply more than they say directly* . . . (a) *"It's comforting,"* he *said. "You'd be surprised how* . . ." It's comforting to the father to be shaved at last. But the words seem to have a larger meaning: it must be comforting to the man to see his son take over this way. The father can surrender himself to his mature, reliable, and loving son. (b) *"You're young,"* his father said, *"to have this happen."* Barry is bigger than most men. We are told early in the story that "four men, roped together, spent a week climbing him—they thought he was Everest." But obviously Barry is bigger than most men because of his heart, his caring, his soul. Would most teenagers shrink away from the starkness and despair of a parent's terminal illness? (c) *"But now the window was full in the beam of the dying sunlight* . . ." It's not only the sunlight which is dying in this story, and it's not only the sun which would soon be gone. This is a very affecting ending for this touching story.

2. **Diction** *is an author's choice of words or phrases, and those words intrinsically contribute to the mood* . . . (a) "With infinite and meticulous care" show how Barry treats his father; (b) "Fleshless and vulnerable" show the seriousness of the father's condition; (c) The love Barry shows for his father is both "unreasoning" and "protective." (d) In one sentence late in the story "the smell of illness" works in contrast to the "perfumed lather." (e) "Taint" may convey the serious illness, but "free of taint" implies that what the son has done overwhelms death.

WRITING WORKSHOP

This extraordinary story is centered on one seemingly simple activity . . .

1. *Observe someone performing an extended action* . . . This activity will help your students realize how crucial closely observed details are to any writing. This assignment is not just arbitrary busy work but is, rather, at the heart of all writing.

2. *Write a prose selection in which you tell about a parent* . . . It's easy to write about tensions between parents and children. For this assignment, urge your students to capture a wholesome and happy time between parent and child.

Guess What? I Almost Kissed My Father Goodnight
Robert Cormier

INTRODUCING THE STORY

The narrator of this story is puzzled by his father. How well do students feel they know their parents? Do they know anything about their parents' past, their hopes and failures? Is it important to know these things?

If some students are familiar with Robert Cormier's books, ask them what they enjoy most about his plots and characters.

RESPONDING TO THE STORY

1. *Why is the narrator surprised at seeing his father . . . ?* Mike's father is a very predictable kind of fellow. Further, Mike sees him in a certain way, and that way doesn't include sitting in the park during the time when he would normally be at work. Ask: Do we all see our parents as predictable people who wouldn't stray from well-established patterns?

2. *"Didn't I fake my way through life most of the time—. . . ."* If students tell the truth in class and not a "half-truth," they'll probably acknowledge that fibbing or telling white lies, or worse, helps them through tough situations. Will some students say that no lie can ever be justified? Get a debate going.

3. *"Even fathers are people." What does Mike's father mean by these words . . . ?* Fathers (or all adults) have the same hopes and fears and dreams and letdowns as young people have. Mike's father is giving a message to Mike: "Don't put me up on a pedestal as some kind of perfect being who never has a doubt. Whatever human feelings you have, I've had them, too, and I still have them." Do students believe that their parents or other adults go through the same kinds of ups and downs as they do? This question ought to provoke a good discussion.

EXPLORING THE AUTHOR'S CRAFT

Figurative language *is language that makes use of comparisons . . .* Your students should be able to find a few more examples of figurative language, such as " . . . her hair a lemon halo in the sun" and "as if I was storing them in my mind like film to develop them later when they'd have meaning for me."

WRITING WORKSHOP

Think of someone whom you know well . . . This should be a major writing activity. If your students can think and write in original language, they will have a jump up on the rest of the world, which rewards people who can communicate clearly and effectively. These written exercises can get your students started on the path toward vivid communication with written language. If students are keeping journals, encourage them to record similes and metaphors, their own as well as those encountered in their readings.

Marigolds
Eugenia Collier

INTRODUCING THE STORY

After reading the first two paragraphs of "Marigolds," students may be asked to recall unusual objects, of beauty or otherwise, found in settings where one would not expect to see them. Why are they memorable? Can students recall their feelings at the time?

RESPONDING TO THE STORY

1. *Why do you think the narrator "leaped furiously into . . . ?"* Humans are animals, and sometimes human behavior seems pretty animalistic. What these young people do to the marigolds is an example. They resent the beauty of the flowers in the midst of squalor, and they see Miss Lottie and John Burke as ripe targets for mischief. Two telling sentences reveal the psychology behind the act: "Perhaps we had some dim notion of what we were, and how little chance we had of being anything else. Otherwise, why would we have been so preoccupied with destruction?" Can your students understand this psychology?

   Can students relate to people who destroy? Probably some of them can. In many classes, I've had boys (rarely girls) talk of wanton destruction "just for fun." Get a discussion going.

2. *Why does the narrator describe "that violent, crazy act . . . ?"* She suddenly feels a sense of responsibility; she sees that her actions have an effect, a horrible result. She has left innocence. "In that humiliating moment I looked beyond myself and into the depths of another person. This was the beginning of compassion, and one cannot have both compassion and innocence."

3. *Do you believe that whole phases of lives can change in moments . . . ?* Those students who might agree with this concept might not want to share the occurrence that convinced them, but try to get some talk going. Your class will never truly work—and truly deal with the "guts" of literature—unless honesty is the watchword, from the first day of the school year.

4. *"Memory is an abstract painting—it does not present things . . ."* These works should be wonderful to share, and you will be startled at what your students produce. Their creations can be part of the curriculum, too, and naturally should be.

EXPLORING THE AUTHOR'S CRAFT

One cannot read this story without feeling as if one has been in this poor, fading town . . . Setting is absolutely essential in this story. We're told about the dust early in the story—"the brown, crumbly dust of late summer"—and we're caught up in the dust and poverty of this town throughout the story. The poverty is the catalyst, we're told, for the violence to the little bit of beauty in the town—Miss Lottie's marigolds. How does Eugenia Collier make us feel this place? She names things, and she is specific. You might have your students go through the story and point out everything that is named, everything tangible.

WRITING WORKSHOP

Capture in words a place you know as vividly as Eugenia Collier . . . Emulating Eugenia Collier is a perfect way to attack this assignment. Students always benefit by seeing models of what they are attempting, so the task for Exploring the Author's Craft above should help them bring alive their own place. Be sure your students use specific details and that the writing appeals to various senses.

Asphalt
Frederick Pollack

INTRODUCING THE STORY

Briefly remind students of "A Private Talk with Holly," "Shaving," and "Guess What? . . ." Ask: How well did the main characters communicate in these stories? If they did communicate well, why did they? Then tell them that this student-written story is about a failure to communicate and ask students to be ready to discuss possible reasons for this failure and to evaluate how well the author succeeds in portraying his characters.

RESPONDING TO THE STORY

1. *"What is the point?"* . . . *What do you see as the point of this story?* The point may be the failure of father and son to communicate, a failure which may be extended to all humans. Interestingly, this award-winning student story was written contemporaneously (in the early 1960s) with Edward Albee's *The Zoo Story* and Samuel Beckett's *Krapp's Last Tape,* both of which are referred to in the story. Both plays are considered to be absurdist, and one of the themes of that dramatic convention is the inability of people to communicate. In "Asphalt" the boy can't relate to his father's past. Father and son haven't seen each other in five months; is that a telling fact?

2. *How do you feel about this father and son and their relationship?* One can only feel sadness; there seems an unbridgeable gap between father and son. Ask: Who seems to be making an effort to forge communication? Does the boy ever make a positive effort?

3. *Why do you think Frederick Pollack entitled his story "Asphalt"?* Asphalt is an appropriate metaphor for the hard, bleak relationship between father and son.

EXPLORING THE AUTHOR'S CRAFT

This writer showed extraordinary skill in making a relationship come alive . . . The length of the students' lists will be a commentary on Frederick Pollack's ability to vividly capture a scene.

WRITING WORKSHOP

A comparison and contrast essay touches upon similarities (comparisons) and differences (contrasts) . . . Ask your students if they can think of occasions when they have had to compare and contrast things—maybe in social studies, maybe in science. Ask them about times when this is done in "real life"—when one is shopping for a certain product, for example, or choosing a college or career.

"Asphalt" and either "Shaving" or "Guess What? I Almost Kissed My Father Goodnight" provide fertile material for practicing comparison and contrast critical thinking skills.

RESPONDING TO PART TWO

1. *In this section, titled "Families and Friends," there are three stories . . .* Ask: Are the three stories primarily about universalities of parent-child relationships, or are they limited to father-son experiences? Can girls in the class see themselves in the stories—maybe even as daughter-father stories, not just daughter-mother stories? Encourage a debate.

2. *In most stories in Part Two, setting plays an active role . . .* Students will have different favorites, no doubt. Can students explain reasons for the most memorable settings and talk about writing techniques?

3. *Analyze the beginnings of the stories in this part . . .* What can the class learn about good writing from the answers given to this question? What is needed to make a good opening for a story?

Part Three
Falling in Love

Her First Ball
Katherine Mansfield

INTRODUCING THE STORY

Have the first part of the story read aloud, stopping to note and explain references that might puzzle students. Assign the rest of the story and ask students to be alert to Leila's fluctuating emotions throughout the story and the reasons for this.

RESPONDING TO THE STORY

1. *Trace the various moods Leila goes through in this story* . . . Early in the story Leila is exhilarated by the excitement of the dance; she can't imagine why the others seemed "indifferent." Soon, after meeting the "old man—fat, with a big bald patch on his head" and dancing with him, her mood is quickly changed; even the music "seemed to change." "Was this first ball only the beginning of her last ball after all?" she wonders. Soon she sobs. But with a new dance, and a new partner, her youthful optimism is restored. She can enjoy the exuberant feelings of her first ball once again. Given Leila's country upbringing and her isolation from social events, her enthusiasm and naïveté at the beginning and end of the story are quite believable.

2. *Did you like Leila? Explain your reaction to her* . . . Tell students that this is the oldest story in the collection; Katherine Mansfield wrote it in 1922. Aside from superficial differences from the world that today's high school students might know, do your students feel that this story is believable? Do they understand Leila's feelings? Are there universal elements in the story? Does one's own background affect one's acceptance or rejection of Leila? Have students think this through and explain what they mean.

EXPLORING THE AUTHOR'S CRAFT

The first person to dance with Leila . . . The first man to dance with her steers "so beautifully." In one paragraph describing his behavior after the dance and as he sits with Leila, the author describes specific actions that capture the man's shyness and nervousness. (He may also be feeling somewhat superior to Leila.)

The fat man is portrayed negatively. In Leila's eyes he is unappealing. His words quickly deflate her excited mood.

Leila reacts positively or at least neutrally (in her delight at the evening) to the first man, and with a kind of revulsion to the second, reactions that reveal her sensitivity to others. In their reactions to Leila, the men are revealed, again, as shy and nervous (the first), and frank but unappealing and ultimately depressing (the second man).

WRITING WORKSHOP

Think of a setting in which two people have just met . . . Every word written in this dialogue must be revelatory of the character. Students may be surprised at how quickly the characters they have created seem to take over the scene and develop a life of their own.

ALTERNATE MEDIA RESPONSE

Choose two speakers to read the dialogue you created . . . After the students have heard the audiocassettes, ask what conclusions the audience has come to about each character.

The Bass, the River and Sheila Mant
W. D. Wetherell

INTRODUCING THE STORY

This might be a good story to have read aloud. If that is done, does the story generate laughter? Often what a teacher thinks is funny is not perceived as humorous by adolescents (and certainly vice versa), but this story does not rely on sophisticated word play, which often tickles teachers. If you want to assign either suggestion under Alternate Media Response, have students prepare ahead of class time.

RESPONDING TO THE STORY

1. *How did you like this story? For once, we have an author who . . .* The simple actions in this story should elicit some laughter from students as they envision that canoe ride.

2. *Why does Sheila Mant appeal to the narrator?* Sheila Mant is exactly the kind of girl who would appeal to this shy, unsophisticated narrator. She is beautiful, older, alluring in many ways, snobbish—just the kind of girl he can never obtain ("all but out of reach"), so he is hopelessly drawn to her.

3. *What kind of person is Sheila? Give a portrait of her . . .* Sheila speaks haughtily. She is in her own world, which, she hopes, will involve a sports cars rather than canoes. Her words are all statements about herself; she never shows any interest in the narrator. Her words reveal her character perfectly.

EXPLORING THE AUTHOR'S CRAFT

Here is a tough analytical question: How does W. D. Wetherell make this story amusing . . . ? Comedy starts with surprise. This story has a great set of contrasts: Sophisticated (or so she believes) Sheila Mant and fishing for bass out of the back of a canoe. Things just *had* to go wrong. Slapstick comedy emerges as Sheila blathers on about her problems with her complexion and the narrator fights the "biggest bass I had ever hooked." If students aspire to write comedy, they must create surprise and great contrasts. In the Marx Brothers' classic comedies the contrast is often between a pompous, straitlaced person and buffoons performing the most lowbrow of anarchic pranks.

WRITING WORKSHOP

It's much easier to see the humor in a painful situation . . . Can your students stand back far enough from their present selves to see some humor in something that happened to them? Can they laugh at themselves as victims in the human comedy? These papers *must* be shared.

ALTERNATE MEDIA RESPONSE

1. *Analyze a current situation comedy on television . . .* Analyzing comedy requires some sophistication. Require that these analyses be precise and not general. Have the reports presented orally and have students discuss whether they agree on the source of the comedy in these shows.

2. *Study videos or reruns of some famous movie and television comedians . . .* It's one thing to laugh at something one reads or sees, but to understand *why* it is or isn't funny is taking matters to an entirely new level. There may be some natural humorists, but most probably have studied other people's success with comedy and know exactly who and what they are emulating. Help your students do the same kind of analysis. Can they see historical precedents for today's comedians?

The Osage Orange Tree
William Stafford

INTRODUCING THE STORY

Since the writing assignment with this story depends somewhat on attention to the setting in "The Osage Orange Tree," parts of which can be used as a model, ask students to be alert to the time and place (setting) as they read.

RESPONDING TO THE STORY

1. *It's a scene we don't see and can only imagine . . .* This question is pure reader response. What do your students think? Evangeline must have felt regret and loss, but there may be other views. Solicit them.

2. *"In a strange town, if you are quiet, no one notices, and some may like you, later."* . . . The wisdom in this sentence has to do with the word *later*. In rural areas people are accepted only after much time and after much proving. See whether your students know this and agree that this is true about any town.

EXPLORING THE AUTHOR'S CRAFT

1. *The term* **imagery** *refers to the sensory details in a literary work . . .* William Stafford, a well-known poet, makes us feel the cold and starkness of this prairie landscape. The passage describing Evangeline's house the only time the narrator actually goes there is vivid in its description of the home's barrenness. The brief description of the Osage orange tree is in some contrast to much of the rest of the story; despite its being a "feeble" tree with thorns, it is "coming into leaf" and there are promises of growth at that tree where the narrator and Evangeline regularly met.

   This story rests not just on its simple plot but also on its atmospherics, and the imagery is crucial.

2. *Analyze what William Stafford did in this story . . .* We care for both the narrator and Evangeline because they are depicted as modest, shy people who have little. They show no meanness despite having had tough, spartan lives. It would be difficult not to root for these two and for their tentative, unexpressed relationship. Get your students talking about how authors can manipulate how we feel about characters and how description of characters' behavior leads us to be sympathetic or unsympathetic toward them.

WRITING WORKSHOP

The setting—"openness, the plains, a big swoop of nothing" and that forlorn house . . . This writing task will help students develop their powers of observation and their ability to be specific. Developing this ability will have broad applications in the future, when critical thinking and the ability to communicate with precision will be highly valuable in the academic world and in the world of work.

Surprised
Catherine Storr

INTRODUCING THE STORY

By now students should be able to discuss their preferences in short stories. Do they prefer to read about situations, people, and settings that are similar to or different from what they know? Are boys' preferences different from girls'? Ask them to think about their preferences in style of writing as well. Tell them that "Surprised," like "The Osage Orange Tree," has almost no dialogue. Ask them to be ready to discuss not only whether "Surprised" would have been more effective with dialogue but what they think of the main character.

RESPONDING TO THE STORY

1. *Is Tossie a recognizable character? Have her feelings . . . been demonstrated by anyone you know?* There are probably people in your class who know a Tossie, or who are a Tossie—people who always build things up too much and who always are crushed, and people who make their emotional roller coaster highly visible as well.

2. *Are Tossie's feelings common to both boys and girls? Explain.* It might be fair to say that there are probably more Tossies who are female than male since our society doesn't always encourage public expressions of emotions among males.

3. *In one of the rare moments in this story when something . . .* Tossie is melodramatic about all aspects of her life, it seems. Her knowing exactly how many weeks and days it has been since she and Jamie broke up reveals the intensity of her awareness of herself and of her emotional life.

4. *According to the narrator's portrait of Tossie . . .* In Tossie's case, one could tell that she was falling in love when she was "very quiet and mysterious" for a while. Then she'd be totally wrapped up in the relationship and "couldn't talk about anything else." Later, when the relationship hit hard times, she'd be at home, quietly suffering, and then finally publicly suffering, warning her sister about the pitfalls of love.

EXPLORING THE AUTHOR'S CRAFT

Of the three main components of a short story . . . In this story setting is least important and character is most important. This story is almost entirely about a character and what makes her tick. Plot hardly figures in at all here. Conflict, if there is one, is between Tossie and the elements in her which she keeps repeating— the tendency to build things up too much and then be crushed. There is minor tension between Tossie and her sister, the narrator, who sees herself as a junior version of her older sister; the narrator fears she'll fall into the same patterns of behavior that Tossie did.

WRITING WORKSHOP

Many country-and-western songs deal with different aspects of love . . . If these aren't corny and if students resist the temptation to do parodies, these might be good. (Some parodies might be good, too.) If students are serious, tell them to emulate the country-and-western songs that play on intense human emotions; Tossie is a good country-and-western song subject because she doesn't hide her emotions.

ALTERNATE MEDIA RESPONSE

Create a TV talk show. Choose an interviewer who should . . . This could work out well if students are willing to be frank; many students will naturally stay mum on this subject, either from lack of experience, from embarrassment, or from a desire to keep personal things private. Choose a talk show host who is good at eliciting comments from his or her peers, someone who is trusted and can draw people out.

I Go Along
Richard Peck

INTRODUCING THE STORY

Review with students the various ways we learn about characters (direct description, what the characters think or say, what others say or think about them, how they act, and the setting and tastes of that character). Ask students to be alert to the methods Richard Peck uses to tell us about his characters.

Students familiar with Peck's novels should be encouraged to talk about their favorite books.

RESPONDING TO THE STORY

1. *Is this story appropriately placed in a section called "Falling in Love"? Explain.* We get little hints in this story of Gene's developing fascination with Sharon, a fascination that occurs all in one evening. ("I've never been this close to her before, so I've never seen the color of her eyes . . . Since it's dark, I take a chance and glance at her . . .")

2. *What do you think the narrator means by the last line?* Maybe this evening has changed Gene. For starters, he's found out that the poems don't have to rhyme and that poets can even look like himself. Gene has also met a girl who sought him out, who wanted to sit next to him on the bus and with him at the poetry reading. The prospects of going back to his regular class "in second period with Marty and Pink and Darla" are depressing to him.

EXPLORING THE AUTHOR'S CRAFT

In some short stories, the main character wrestles with physical . . . This story is quite short. Is there enough time for author Richard Peck—himself a poet—to create a well-developed main character? Does Gene's "transformation" ring true? Could all of this happen on one school field trip? Considering the fragmentation and intensity of teenagers' lives, this is quite possible. We learn about Gene's alienation from his own class almost immediately. When he volunteers to go with the advanced class on this trip, we see he is already searching for something beyond the Martys and Pinks and Darlas of the world, even if Gene doesn't quite realize it.

WRITING WORKSHOP

1. *Write about the next day in the narrator's life from Gene's point of view.* No doubt Sharon will somehow appear in these narrations. How the stories proceed will tell you more about your students and how they see life today—or perhaps how they might wish it to be—than you could ever receive from a straight-forward essay.

2. *In a paragraph or two, fill in some additional details of Gene's life . . .* This is a great activity to engender thinking. The assignment "lets the students go," based on their knowledge of people their age, and they have great knowledge of this topic. Tell students to be sure that they can justify with material from the story their speculations about other aspects of Gene's life.

Broken Chain
Gary Soto

INTRODUCING THE STORY

Ask students to list five things about themselves that a short story writer might use to characterize them. Possibilities include taste in clothing and music, where they live, what they carry with them, hair style, chief worry, greatest accomplishment.

These lists need not be shared, or they may be read by you without names attached. Ask: Would any items on the lists have to be explained to someone who lived one hundred years ago and who suddenly reappeared? Ask students to note as they read "Broken Chain" all the references to Alfonso's world and how those references contribute to the reader's understanding and interest in the story.

RESPONDING TO THE STORY

1. *Does Gary Soto have it right about being in seventh grade . . . ?* The first six paragraphs contain vivid details of what matters to Alfonso—how he looks and how girls might respond. Have your students' lists read aloud; does everyone agree that Alfonso is a classic case of a seventh grader getting interested in romance?

2. *What other aspects of being in seventh grade does the author understand . . . ?* All of the details about Alfonso's obsession with his looks ring true for young people. His embarrassment about making mistakes is believable. His range of emotions from outright despair to ecstasy ("She placed her hand over his, and it felt like love") would be recognized by psychologists or psychiatrists who work with adolescents. What other aspects of Alfonso's life do your students see as believable? Do your students find any details of Alfonso's life that don't ring true? Trust your students' responses about the world they know; they are experts on this topic.

EXPLORING THE AUTHOR'S CRAFT

This story is filled with the "stuff" of daily life . . . Soto evokes a world whose characters are concerned with the immediate moment, with happenings that affect them directly. Theirs is not a world of interest in the evening news or of much thought of another person, unless that person is the object of romance. All in all, Gary Soto recalls well what it's like to be young.

WRITING WORKSHOP

In Gary Soto's California, Alfonso . . . This exercise will help students realize how important details are. Have some fun with this as your students talk about the popular world around them—the world of clothing, of food, of *any* kind of shopping, of the music they listen to, the television they watch, and the slang they use. De-emphasize plot in this exercise.

And Summer Is Gone
Susie Kretschmer

INTRODUCING THE STORY

This is one of the two stories in *Coming of Age* written by a female writer who creates a male narrator. ("Sucker" is the other story.) Ask students to consider as they read how well the author has succeeded at this.

RESPONDING TO THE STORY

1. *Is it believable that a boy and girl at age twelve . . . ?* Student responses will be totally based on their own experiences. Ask: after about age eleven or twelve, can a boy and a girl be really good friends without romance—or the possibility of it—entering in somewhere?

2. *Did you sympathize with the narrator's plight? Why or why not?* Almost everyone has had friendships change, and some have been hurt in the process. Will your students be able to talk about their hurts? It depends on the degree of openness and trust in the class; sometimes in the same year, with the same teacher teaching the same way, some classes come together and some don't. In the ones that do, topics such as this one can be discussed very effectively.

EXPLORING THE AUTHOR'S CRAFT

Identify two places in the story where you feel the author . . . The author might have included a scene describing the beginning of freshman year and showing the final separation between Amy and the narrator rather than telling about it. By including a scene capturing the awkward summer between seventh and eighth grades, she might have skillfully let us realize that some tension and some distancing were developing in the relationship. Instead, Susie Kretschmer (a high school student when she wrote the story) summarized the events in these two time periods. Dramatizing a scene makes it much more vivid and authentic than a mere summary does, as illustrated by the story's last scene at the art exhibit at the local library, which enables readers to reach their own conclusions rather than being told what to believe.

WRITING WORKSHOP

1. *"All of them had names that ended in -i, and they all . . ."* This should be fun for your students and revealing for you. If some students attended a different school the previous year, they might compare and contrast customs between the two schools.

2. *Author Susie Kretschmer created a male first-person narrator . . .* These papers will have to be shared, and the listeners can comment on how authentic the first-person voices seem to be. The group work in advance of writing can help writers get focused and avoid silliness in creating the persona of a character of the opposite sex. The best papers will be the ones that strike the audience as totally believable.

RESPONDING TO PART THREE

1. *"Her First Ball" was written over seventy years ago . . .* After students have moved beyond some of the outmoded parts, they can discuss what is universal in the story. Perhaps the idea of infatuation with the notion of romance, infatuation with happiness and being exposed to something new in life (as Leila was with the idea of the dance), is universal, as is having to meet odd characters who have an effect on us—as the rather pathetic fat man did on Leila.

2. **Suspense** *is the condition of being uncertain about how a story will end . . .* Although none of these stories relies solely on suspense to keep us reading, we do wonder whether the narrator can win over Sheila Mant, and whether Alfonso will get to go bike riding with Sandra. We wonder how Gene will react to the poetry reading, and we fear for the outcome of "The Osage Orange Tree." In "Surprised" we're not surprised to see Tossie repeatedly falling into her old behavior patterns, however.

3. **Style** *refers to the way an author uses language . . .* Remind your students how often in life we all have to use the critical thinking skills of comparison and contrast. Have your students brainstorm in groups and make lists of similarities or differences before they actually begin to write. A good oral presentation or short paper on this topic will be an excellent way to assess how well your students truly know and have internalized these seven stories.

   As an additional exercise, you may want to choose isolated paragraphs from other Mansfield, Peck, Rawlings, Cisneros, and Cormier stories, read them aloud, and ask students to match the paragraphs with their authors.

Part Four
Out in the World

A Visit of Charity
Eudora Welty

INTRODUCING THE STORY

Have someone define *charity*. (One definition is "generosity or goodwill toward the needy.") Ask students to read to discover whether the visit of charity in the story benefitted either the main character, Marian, or the recipients of the charity.

RESPONDING TO THE STORY

1. *"How old are you?" Marian breathed. Now she could see the old woman . . .* This seems to be Marian's initiation into a world of illness. She is discovering more of the world than her family or school has taught her in her fourteen years. Part of coming of age is learning about the bad things in the world; illness and mental dysfunction are some of these bad things, and today Marian is having her eyes opened.

2. *Before Marian has spoken more than three full sentences . . .* The reader has been introduced to a girl who seems to be on a "visit of charity" more to score points for the Campfire Girls than to help the infirm. "I have to pay a visit to some old lady," conveys it all. The words *have* and *some* stress Marian's lack of commitment to this project.

3. *Why do you suppose the author ends the story as she does?* Marian retrieves the apple that she has left under the prickly shrub on her way into the Old Ladies' Home; she shouts to the bus driver, "Wait for me!," jumps on the bus, and takes a bite from her apple. Readers may make several inferences about the ending. Certainly Marian feels relief, and, like many young people, perhaps she can move rapidly on with her life, forgetting the shock of what she has witnessed. At any rate, she seems unable to empathize with the obvious plight of the nursing home inhabitants. She may, however, be affected forever by the event, though she seems not to be when she departs. Discuss whether the apple is a symbol. Deconstructionist critics may say that the apple she has bitten into indicates the loss of innocence for Marian. Ask: Who benefitted from Marian's charitable visit? How does the answer to this question help define the theme of the story?

EXPLORING THE AUTHOR'S CRAFT

"A Visit of Charity" is told from the **third-person point of view** . . .

1. *What does the hallway of the Home feel and smell like to Marian?* The place is not pleasant; linoleum is loose and the hall smells musty, "like the interior of a clock." This simile is most apt for a home for the elderly, where time ticks away for the residents.

2. *What does the detail of the nurse's reading . . . ?* It is most incongruous that the nurse should be reading *Field and Stream,* a magazine whose readership must be 98 percent male. Marian is so busy trying to get out that she does nothing more than notice the magazine's name, but the reader can react in surprise to the title.

3. *What is the author's purpose in having the two old women in constant disagreement . . . ?* Marian is being introduced, against her will, to a world of dementia and illogic. The two old women must be constantly at odds to heighten the tension in the room. The reader sees that they are mentally ill; Marian is just dumbfounded and scared.

WRITING WORKSHOP

Write a journal entry as Marian might have written it after her visit . . . What will your students write? Will Marian be intense and describe forthrightly everything she saw? Maybe not. Maybe she will be somewhat distracted, as she seems to be when she goes back to her apple upon leaving. Welty never really lets us see Marian reacting except when she tries to escape. But notice that Marian doesn't run out screaming or complain to the nurse at the desk. And when she bites into that apple, we're not quite sure what to think. Be sure your students can justify the tone they create in their journal entries.

A Veil of Water
Amy Boesky

INTRODUCING THE STORY

Tell students they will have to make a number of inferences as they read this student-written story, for the author is not explicit in many details.

RESPONDING TO THE STORY

1. *What has happened to the characters in this story? . . . Explain.* There must have been a shocking and sudden death of both parents, perhaps in a car accident. "I want to talk to you about what happened," the aunt tells the narrator. The narrator resists the information: "What happened? Nothing happened," she says "stubbornly." The narrator in her innocent voice tells us that "in the cartoons the animals and people are always getting hurt, but in the next scene they are better again." People who were hurt and are only vaguely referred to in this story won't be getting better again, we sense. Ask students to find other clues to the various mysteries of the story. What *has* gone on?

2. *What clues are there about the ages of the narrator and her brother?* We know that the narrator and her brother are young. Her cousins pull at her hair. She watches cartoons on television and refers to them in the present tense, as if she regularly watches them. When she says of her uncle, "He does not undress me," the statement implies that she might have expected him to, so she is probably under ten or so. Ask your students to look for more clues in this marvelously crafted story which was written by a high school senior.

EXPLORING THE AUTHOR'S CRAFT

1. *Another story with a bird as a symbol! . . .* The bird is intentionally black since the nightmare involves death. As stated earlier, the cartoons portray a view of life unlike the one the girl and her brother are discovering.

2. *A* **motif** *is an idea, element, incident, or object . . .* The motif is water. The aquarium was an important place in the narrator's father's life, both with his own brother and with his children. Everyone used to look at the world through water. Now the narrator is crying and "my eyes are blinded with my tears. The world looks different suddenly. I am seeing it through water, and it will never look the same again." Water in the form of tears is an appropriate motif in this story of reaction to tragedy in life. Point out that a motif differs from a symbol in that it does not stand for something else as a symbol does.

WRITING WORKSHOP

Amy Boesky, who wrote this story as a senior in high school, hadn't experienced . . . Warn your students not to engage in wild speculation—it is difficult for an adolescent to think ten days ahead, much less ten years—but to realistically project themselves and their personalities into the future. Given who they are now, what might be a logical conclusion about what they will be like in ten years? Then they must make the diary entry vivid and specific and somehow consistent with the person they are now.

ALTERNATE MEDIA RESPONSE

Illustrate a moment in this story that you find especially gripping or dramatic. Share these. One of the goals in the English/language arts class is to help students communicate with others, both orally and in writing. Here's a chance for those students who have created an illustration to show it to the class, to elicit comments, and to talk about how the work was created. Let your classroom be the forum for all kinds of communication and sharing; I guarantee that all the traditional "English classroom goals" will still be accomplished—and probably more successfully than in the traditional "teacher-centered" class.

Teenage Wasteland
Anne Tyler

INTRODUCING THE STORY

Discuss the denotations and connotations of the word *wasteland* and have students speculate about what the author might mean by the story title. Ask them to read to discover how accurate their predictions are and to be ready to discuss the appropriateness of the title.

RESPONDING TO THE STORY

1. *How did you respond to this story? Are you sympathetic . . . ?* Take a vote in your class. How many like Donny and how many don't? Then get the discussion going. Students must base their comments on the text and on their knowledge of human nature. "Teenage Wasteland" should be one of the most provocative stories in this book for today's adolescents.

2. *Why do you think you responded as you did . . . ?* Reader response theory says that we respond in certain ways because of our own experiences. Get your students to talk about both this question and the first question about the story because the questions go together.

3. *Why do you think the author titled this story "Teenage Wasteland"?* "Teenage Wasteland" works as a wonderful title for this story. Donny listens to the Who's song of this title. Donny's father wonders if Donny and the other people at Cal's home epitomize this theme. Does the author mean it descriptively or ironically? (See Exploring the Author's Craft.)

EXPLORING THE AUTHOR'S CRAFT

What is the author's attitude toward her subject, her tone . . . ? Various positions can be supported with evidence from the text. Tyler skewers everyone—Donny, his parents, tutor Cal, and the other young people at Cal's home who "looked like hoodlums." This question might lead to a good debate that relies on the debaters referring constantly to the text. The debate thus becomes oral literary criticism.

WRITING WORKSHOP

Try to imagine a different ending for this story . . . This story didn't have to end this way, of course. Yes, they are Anne Tyler's characters, but your students can direct those characters any way they wish. Have students share their various endings, and take the discussion to a conversation about endings in general; what must a good ending do? How consistent must it be with the rest of the story?

Initiation
Sylvia Plath

INTRODUCING THE STORY

Talk about the purposes of an initiation into a club, fraternity, sorority, gang, or some other group, especially an initiation that requires the initiant to perform embarrassing, frightening, or even dangerous acts. Does anyone benefit from such initiations? What is the motive behind organizations or clubs that strive to maintain exclusivity? Have students read to find out how one girl outwits the members of a sorority.

RESPONDING TO THE STORY

1. *Why was the "part of initiation that I figured out myself" . . . ?* The "worst part, the hardest part" wasn't surviving the initiation pranks. The hardest part was figuring out that she didn't have to be in the sorority, that her life might be better—and that she could still befriend Tracy—if she weren't in the sorority. She would shock the sorority by declining their invitation; but she would be true to herself.

2. *How do you interpret the story's last line?* This last line can be interpreted in various ways. This decision, this event, might be Millicent's initiation into the adult world, away from the games and vicious competition of high school. She

could "go along" and join the very popular, highly prestigious sorority, or she could take a stand and be her own person. She was about to become her own heather bird.

3. *Do you agree with Millicent's decision not to join . . . ?* This will provoke some debate. It might be easy to say that each of us would do exactly what Millicent did, but would we? Some students will get emotionally involved in this question because they may have faced very similar situations involving decisions about following the crowd or making value judgments. Let your students talk this one out.

EXPLORING THE AUTHOR'S CRAFT

A **flashback** *is an interruption in a chronological narrative that shows something that happened before that point in the story . . .*

1. *Where does the flashback in "Initiation" begin and end?* The flashback begins with the sixth paragraph and includes virtually the entire story, right up to the paragraph near the end that states, "Seated now on the woodpile in Betsy Johnson's cellar . . ." Now we are back to the "present tense" of the story, Millicent is about to be accepted into the sorority, and she is about to make her statement.

2. *What does the flashback in this story accomplish?* The flashback shows the reader how Millicent's thinking has evolved over the days leading up to the climactic Rat Court. We are told early in the story that Millicent had decided to "revolt," so her decision not to join the sorority really isn't a surprise. The heart of the story is the depiction of events leading to Millicent's decision.

WRITING WORKSHOP

1. *Create a one- or two-paragraph response . . .* What do these people think and do? Are they shocked? Angry? Help students get the voices of each of these four people just right.

2. *Author Sylvia Plath used two similes in this story to reflect . . .* Give your students time to write in class, and demand silence in the room. Have students review the story and pick a section they wish to express in a simile. Put a number of the similes on the chalkboard or type them up and produce multiple copies so that students can see the wording.

Betty
Margaret Atwood

INTRODUCING THE STORY

Writers are often asked where they get their ideas for stories. Ask students to think about possible answers to this question; then ask them to be ready to discuss the techniques the author uses to reveal character. They may want to make notes as they read.

RESPONDING TO THE STORY

We learn every day, . . . from what is around us . . .

1. *Write a statement explaining what the narrator learned . . .* The narrator learns that there are other ways of life than those of the city. She learns from the couple upstairs that physical violence can occur between people. She learns from Betty and Fred countless lessons about varieties in human beings. She learns from Nan about being a teenager and the customs of that world, and so on, throughout this story. Like all of us, the narrator is constantly taking in the world around her. Your students' lists will contain many diverse instances of learning.

2. *Explain what you think the author means by the last paragraph.* This is a very rich story. The last paragraph seems to say that Fred, despite surface charm, was a person not to like. There are many indications of this in the story, including the unexplained look of the girl outside the store. Betty, on the other hand, still haunts the narrator. She is mysterious: "I would like to show her this story I have told about her and ask her if any of it is true." Betty, one senses, will always be a part of the narrator's life.

EXPLORING THE AUTHOR'S CRAFT

In this story we come to know a number of people, each of whom . . . Students can work in groups on this. Try to guarantee that a good variety of characters are written about, even the so-called minor characters. What can we learn about characterization from this story? Characterization is created by the details, by the specifics, by the anecdotes. All of us as people are revealed in our behavior, in the anecdotes about us.

WRITING WORKSHOP

1. *Tell about the learning you have done outside of school . . .* This should be a rewarding activity, both for the students who reflect on their own lives and for the class which hears about this learning. It will become clear that most if not all of your students have the stuff of fiction in their own lives. Maybe this book has helped them realize that, and maybe this book has given them certain techniques to help them communicate their stories effectively, whether in prose or poetry.

2. *Betty seems a very ordinary person; yet, she is the title character . . .* This could be a major paper for your students, who will have to go back to the text—perhaps repeatedly—in order to find evidence for their statements.

   The text will show that Betty is a thoroughly decent person but one who "didn't grasp things very well." She probably pursued Fred more than he pursued her. She didn't catch on, even though there were probably clues, that he was drifting from her and about to abandon her. She's warm and she laughs and she cares, but she is utterly in shock when Fred, the only subject she ever talks about, runs off. When she returns to the narrator's life four years later, Betty is trying on a new identity; she wants to be called Elizabeth. She is a rather pathetic figure, someone who had no insight into her own life. That she dies of a brain tumor is the final unfair blow to this pitiable person.

On the Late Bus
Susan Engberg

INTRODUCING THE STORY

Put the following quotation on the chalkboard and elicit opinions about its meaning.

Be patient toward all that is unsolved in your heart, and try to live the questions themselves.

—Rainer Maria Rilke

Tell students that the main character in "On the Late Bus" faces a number of unsolved questions involving her divorced parents and her place in the world. Have the class read to discover how Alison deals with these questions.

RESPONDING TO THE STORY

1. *Explain how the life situation of the girl has contributed to her mood. Be specific.*
Alison's father has remarried and started a second family, and her mother has
found a boyfriend. The narrator is in the middle (a situation some of your students
may be able to identify with), and she feels unwanted and ill at ease with either
parent. This situation has caused Alison to become depressed and unhappy with
herself.

2. *Although the girl resents the man who is with her on the bus . . .* The man is
"goin' from one daughter to t'other. Neither one wants their old pa." Alison
is in this exact position with her parents.

3. *Is the ending of the story optimistic or pessimistic? Explain.* Although much
of the story is gloomy, the ending is not. First, both the man and Alison are
eating. "Oh, lordy, I always feel better when I'm eating," he tells her. Alison,
who has eaten nothing all day, seems to feel better too. In the last three paragraphs
she has the moon on her side of the bus and, most important, she has an idea
of her own; she's *not* a meaningless person. The idea says something about not
being powerless in life, about being able to do more in life than make "trouble."

4. *Why do you think the author ends the story . . . ?* Alison may be not used to
having ideas of her own. She has come to believe that she just messes up other
people's lives. This sudden idea in her head tells her that "if people could turn
on the trouble, they could make other things happen, too, besides trouble." She
can choose how she feels and can direct her own life. Suddenly, she feels
worthwhile.

EXPLORING THE AUTHOR'S CRAFT

How does the moon function as a symbol here . . . ? About midway through the
story we meet the moon: "Well, at least she had had the window and heard the
far-away, matter-of-fact music of the geese and seen the full moon, with its gigantic
eyes looking back at her." The moon is, at the least, a neutral object; Alison doesn't
cause trouble for it, as she is convinced she causes trouble for everything else she
comes in contact with. Later in the story, as the moon is coming up the next night,
"she didn't think she had ever seen it so close and so big." The moon is now a
beneficent figure in this story, and Alison needs such a companion. Near the story's
end Alison has the "moon to look at while she chewed, the watchful moon. Last
night, tonight, this feeling of being seen was something new. She had a new secret,
the strength of the moon, looking at her." The moon, a sort of talisman, helps her
through these difficult days and leads her, one might say, to being able to have
her life-saving insight at the story's end.

WRITING WORKSHOP

"Other people always stirred things up." *In this story we learn about . . .* Again, try to guide your students into showing and not telling; help them recreate life on the page. "A Visit of Charity" by Eudora Welty is perhaps the best model of that technique; Welty shows or implies everything and never editorializes.

A Walk to the Jetty
Jamaica Kincaid

INTRODUCING THE STORY

Although many students may not have experienced situations similar to the narrator's, they should be able to empathize with her feelings about leaving all that is familiar. Do students react to major changes in their lives with exhilaration or fear— or both? What kinds of changes in life produce the strongest emotions? Ask students to be ready to express the theme of this story, either verbally or through an artistic medium.

RESPONDING TO THE STORY

It is difficult to read Jamaica Kincaid's story without . . . Everyone has had separations. This story should strike chords in all your students, and in you, too. See what reactions you get in various art forms.

EXPLORING THE AUTHOR'S CRAFT

Sometimes being a good writer is just having the willingness and patience . . . Do most students list the same sense impressions, ideas, or feelings? Most likely there will be a good variety of listings, and perhaps they will be revelatory of the reader's own interests and feelings.

WRITING WORKSHOP

The narrator of this story describes her room . . . Let "A Walk to the Jetty" be a model for your students' descriptions. Encourage students not only to describe their place, but, by making it vivid, to evoke in the reader deep memories of the reader's own place. This is, of course, what many writers achieve.

ALTERNATE MEDIA RESPONSE

This story should have evoked many feelings . . . As the works are shared with the class, see whether fellow students can sense the feeling being expressed before the artist himself or herself comments or shares the title of the work.

RESPONDING TO PART FOUR

1. *Being out in the world involves contacts with persons . . .* Marian in "A Visit of Charity" sees behavior she probably hasn't seen before. She stands in that room at the Old Ladies' Home befuddled and frightened, and finally she escapes. Millicent in "Initiation" meets a world that she doesn't want to accept. To join the sorority would mean an important social foundation, but she'd rather be her own person. Marian, in essence, runs from something unpleasant, and Millicent stands up to it.

2. *Leaving one's childhood home is a necessary part of growing up . . .* Donny leaves home in "Teenage Wasteland" as an unhappy person, escaping things he probably couldn't articulate. Annie John in "A Walk to the Jetty" leaves home very willingly, but she still has sentimental attachments to the place that has been her whole life. The mother in "Teenage Wasteland" has been ripped apart by her son's behavior over a long period of time. She has no idea where her son is. The mother in "A Walk to the Jetty" accepts her daughter's leaving and knows where she will be. She says to her daughter, "It doesn't matter what you do or where you go, I'll always be your mother and this will always be your home."

3. *The mood or atmosphere of "On the Late Bus" is quite different from . . .* "On the Late Bus" might be described as a forlorn story, or even a bitter story, despite its hopeful ending. "A Walk to the Jetty" is melancholy, because Annie John has such mixed feelings. "On the Late Bus" is definitely a harsher story than "A Walk to the Jetty." Encourage students to find or think of synonyms for the words *unhappy* or *sad* when describing these stories.

4. *Which author in Part Four would you most like to meet and talk with and why?* I'd like to know the answers to this one. Share responses in class.

A final thought: Reading all the stories one more time as I have prepared this *Teacher's Manual,* I am struck by one thought: I think that *Coming of Age* not only is *about* youth and adolescence but that the book actually *simulates* the age. There is such diversity of situations and problems and ideas and feelings in these pages that all the variables of adolescence have been captured in the book. That is my hope, in any case.

NTC LANGUAGE ARTS BOOKS

Business Communication
Business Communication Today! *Thomas & Fryar*
Handbook for Business Writing, *Baugh, Fryar, & Thomas*
Meetings: Rules & Procedures, *Pohl*

Dictionaries
British/American Language Dictionary, *Moss*
NTC's Classical Dictionary, *Room*
NTC's Dictionary of Changes in Meaning, *Room*
NTC's Dictionary of Debate, *Hanson*
NTC's Dictionary of Literary Terms, *Morner & Rausch*
NTC's Dictionary of Theatre and Drama Terms, *Mobley*
NTC's Dictionary of Word Origins, *Room*
NTC's Spell It Right Dictionary, *Downing*
Robin Hyman's Dictionary of Quotations

Essential Skills
Building Real Life English Skills, *Starkey & Penn*
English Survival Series, *Maggs*
Essential Life Skills, *Starkey & Penn*
Essentials of English Grammar, *Baugh*
Essentials of Reading and Writing English Series
Grammar for Use, *Hall*
Grammar Step-by-Step, *Pratt*
Guide to Better English Spelling, *Furness*
How to be a Rapid Reader, *Redway*
How to Improve Your Study Skills, *Coman & Heavers*
NTC Skill Builders
Reading by Doing, *Simmons & Palmer*
Developing Creative & Critical Thinking, *Boostrom*
303 Dumb Spelling Mistakes, *Downing*
TIME: We the People, *ed. Schinke-Llano*
Vocabulary by Doing, *Beckert*

Genre Literature
The Detective Story, *Schwartz*
The Short Story & You, *Simmons & Stern*
Sports in Literature, *Emra*
You and Science Fiction, *Hollister*

Journalism
Getting Started in Journalism, *Harkrider*
Journalism Today! *Ferguson & Patten*
Publishing the Literary Magazine, *Klaiman*
UPI Stylebook, *United Press International*

Language, Literature, and Composition
An Anthology for Young Writers, *Meredith*
The Art of Composition, *Meredith*
Creative Writing, *Mueller & Reynolds*

Handbook for Practical Letter Writing, *Baugh*
How to Write Term Papers and Reports, *Baugh*
Literature by Doing, *Tchudi & Yesner*
Lively Writing, *Schrank*
Look, Think & Write, *Leavitt & Sohn*
Poetry by Doing, *Osborn*
World Literature, *Rosenberg*
Write to the Point! *Morgan*
The Writer's Handbook, *Karls & Szymanski*
Writing by Doing, *Sohn & Enger*
Writing in Action, *Meredith*

Media Communication
Getting Started in Mass Media, *Beckert*
Photography in Focus, *Jacobs & Kokrda*
Television Production Today! *Kirkham*
Understanding Mass Media, *Schrank*
Understanding the Film, *Bone & Johnson*

Mythology
The Ancient World, *Sawyer & Townsend*
Mythology and You, *Rosenberg & Baker*
Welcome to Ancient Greece, *Millard*
Welcome to Ancient Rome, *Millard*
World Mythology, *Rosenberg*

Speech
Activities for Effective Communication, *LiSacchi*
The Basics of Speech, *Galvin, Cooper, & Gordon*
Contemporary Speech, *HopKins & Whitaker*
Dynamics of Speech, *Myers & Herndon*
Getting Started in Public Speaking, *Prentice & Payne*
Listening by Doing, *Galvin*
Literature Alive! *Gamble & Gamble*
Person to Person, *Galvin & Book*
Public Speaking Today! *Prentice & Payne*
Speaking by Doing, *Buys, Sill, & Beck*

Theatre
Acting & Directing, *Grandstaff*
The Book of Cuttings for Acting & Directing, *Cassady*
The Book of Scenes for Acting Practice, *Cassady*
The Dynamics of Acting, *Snyder & Drumsta*
An Introduction to Modern One-Act Plays, *Cassady*
An Introduction to Theatre and Drama, *Cassady & Cassady*
Play Production Today! *Beck et al.*
Stagecraft, *Beck*

For a current catalog and information about our complete line
of language arts books, write:
National Textbook Company
a division of NTC Publishing Group
4255 West Touhy Avenue
Lincolnwood (Chicago), Illinois 60646-1975 U.S.A.